To Parents, Grandparents, and Other Caring Adults...

YolandaBaby: A Pooch Finds Her Purpose
This is a feelings book. Children will identify with the dog being teased and bullied.

YolandaBaby meets feelings of insecurity head-on as we follow her story from the racetrack to the rescue farm to adoption with a family. During her struggle to discover her true calling, she experiences heartache and fear, but also learns the power of friendship, belonging, and love. The book's background colors change to reflect YolandaBaby's growing happiness.

Talking Tips from YolandaBaby and Jo Ann
While reading the story, ask questions about how YolandaBaby feels.

- **Page 4** speaks of bullies. Ask, "How do you feel when someone is unkind to you?"

- **Page 12** is an opportunity to talk about fears, being different, being chosen last.

- **Page 14** shows that positive comments by authority figures build self-esteem. Ask, "Who makes you feel good about yourself? How does it make you feel?"

- **Page 20** introduces unconditional love. Ask, "Who loves you?"

- **Page 22** shows how YolandaBaby bonds with a new family and friends. Ask, "Who are your friends? How do they support you? When you are with them, how do you feel?"

Wrap-Up Questions
shared by Lou & Diane Tice, The Pacific Institute, Seattle, WA

- 1) Focus on positive accomplishments of the day by asking, "What did you do today that you are proud of?"

- 2) Begin to set up a positive tomorrow by asking, "What are you looking forward to tomorrow?"

Remember, words spoken today will stay with children for a lifetime.

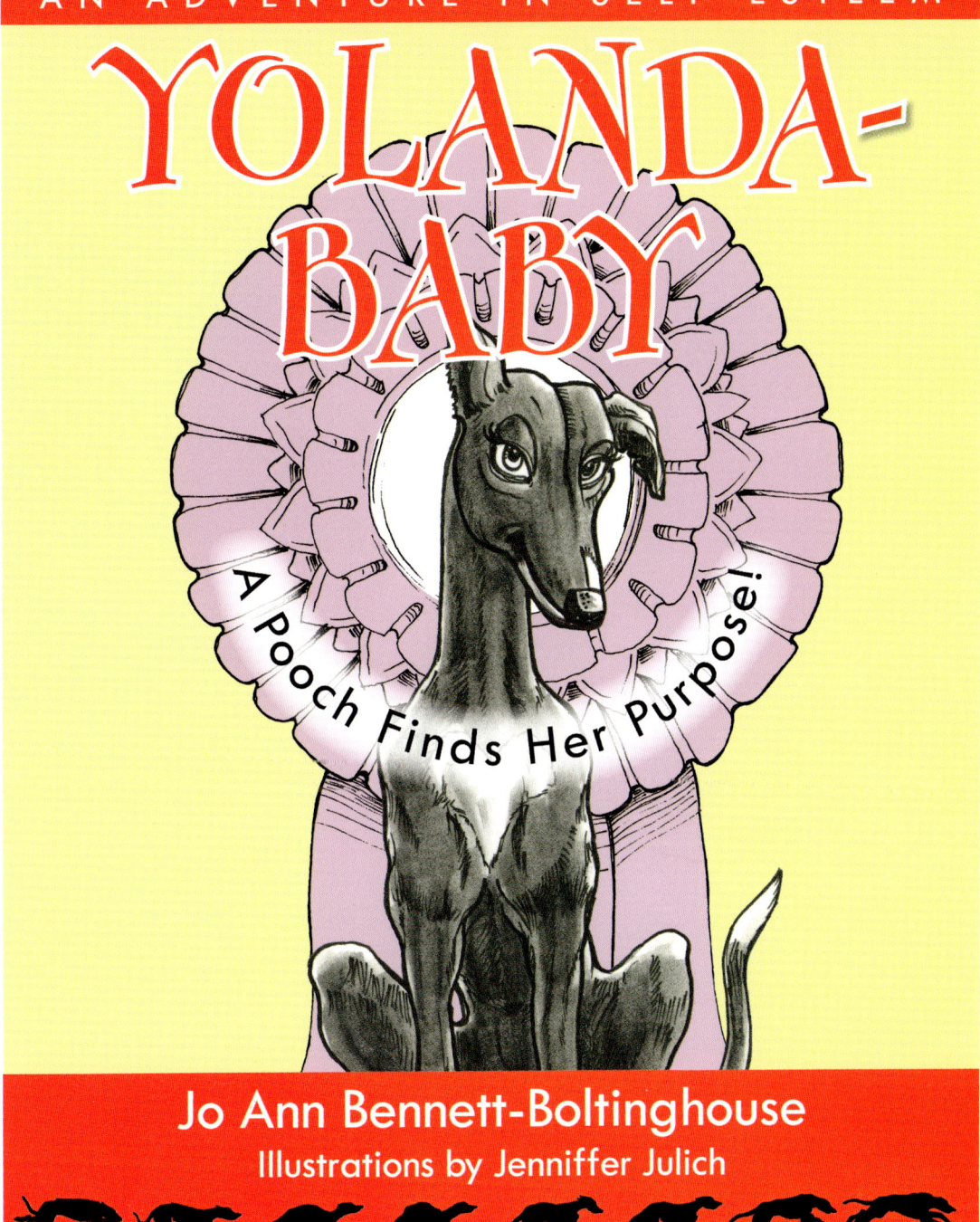

AN ADVENTURE IN SELF-ESTEEM

YOLANDA-BABY

A Pooch Finds Her Purpose!

Jo Ann Bennett-Boltinghouse

Illustrations by Jenniffer Julich

The Ginger Press
Omaha, Nebraska

Copyright © 2006 Jo Ann Bennett-Boltinghouse

All rights reserved. No part of this book may be reproduced or transmitted in any form or by any means, electronic or mechanical, including photocopying, recording, or by any information storage and retrieval system, without permission in writing from the publisher.

Published by The Ginger Press
P.O. Box 45753
Omaha, NE 68145-0753

Publisher's Cataloging-in-Publication Data
Bennett-Boltinghouse, Jo Ann.

YolandaBaby : a pooch finds her purpose : an adventure in self-esteem / Jo Ann Bennett-Boltinghouse; illustrator Jenniffer Julich. — Omaha, NE : Ginger Press, 2006.

p. ; cm.
You will follow YolandaBaby in her struggle to discover her purpose in life as she learns the power of love.

ISBN: 0-9785151-0-2
ISBN13: 978-0-9785151-0-2

1. Self-esteem. 2. Success. I. Julich, Jenniffer, ill. II. Title.

BF697.5.S46 2006
158.1—dc22   2006924876

Illustrations, book and cover design by Jenniffer Julich
Layout and composition of interior and cover by Eric Tufford

Printed in Singapore
10 09 08 07 06 • 5 4 3 2 1

Acknowledgements

I want to thank:

🐾 Carol Johns Corey for her continual caring support and personal friendship,

🐾 the entire Jenkins Group for their professional advice and guidance — Bob, Nikki, Leah, Kim, Jenniffer, Eric and everyone else who had a hand in this project,

🐾 my many friends who read, proofed, and provided feedback as the book unfolded,

🐾 Rory Goree' and all the Greyhound Adoption Groups that have supported this book and project,

🐾 Donna and Jim Lovely, for without them we would have never known YolandaBaby,

🐾 Dr. Lisa Pattison and Lou & Diane Tice for their professional contributions to the parental tutorial,

🐾 the Roger Barnett family for their encouragement for this project and to Roger himself for inspiring me to take charge of my health so I can continue my life's work,

🐾 my staff, Mary, Anna Mae, and Linda for their many hours of critiquing and proofing.

Dedication

This book is dedicated to all children in the hope that they may grow up to "be the best at whatever they choose to be," with a positive attitude and healthy self-esteem.

I'd also like to thank my family for their continued love, support and encouragement as I continue the project "Self-Esteem"!

Hi! My name is YolandaBaby.
I am a greyhound running in yet another race.

Can you find me?

I am a black-haired dog with a white spot on my nose and another on my chest.

You will not find me in front.
I am not even in the middle.

I am trying to run really, really fast,

but I will come in last place... again!

Greyhounds are usually fast dogs. I am not very fast. Some dogs are just better than others.

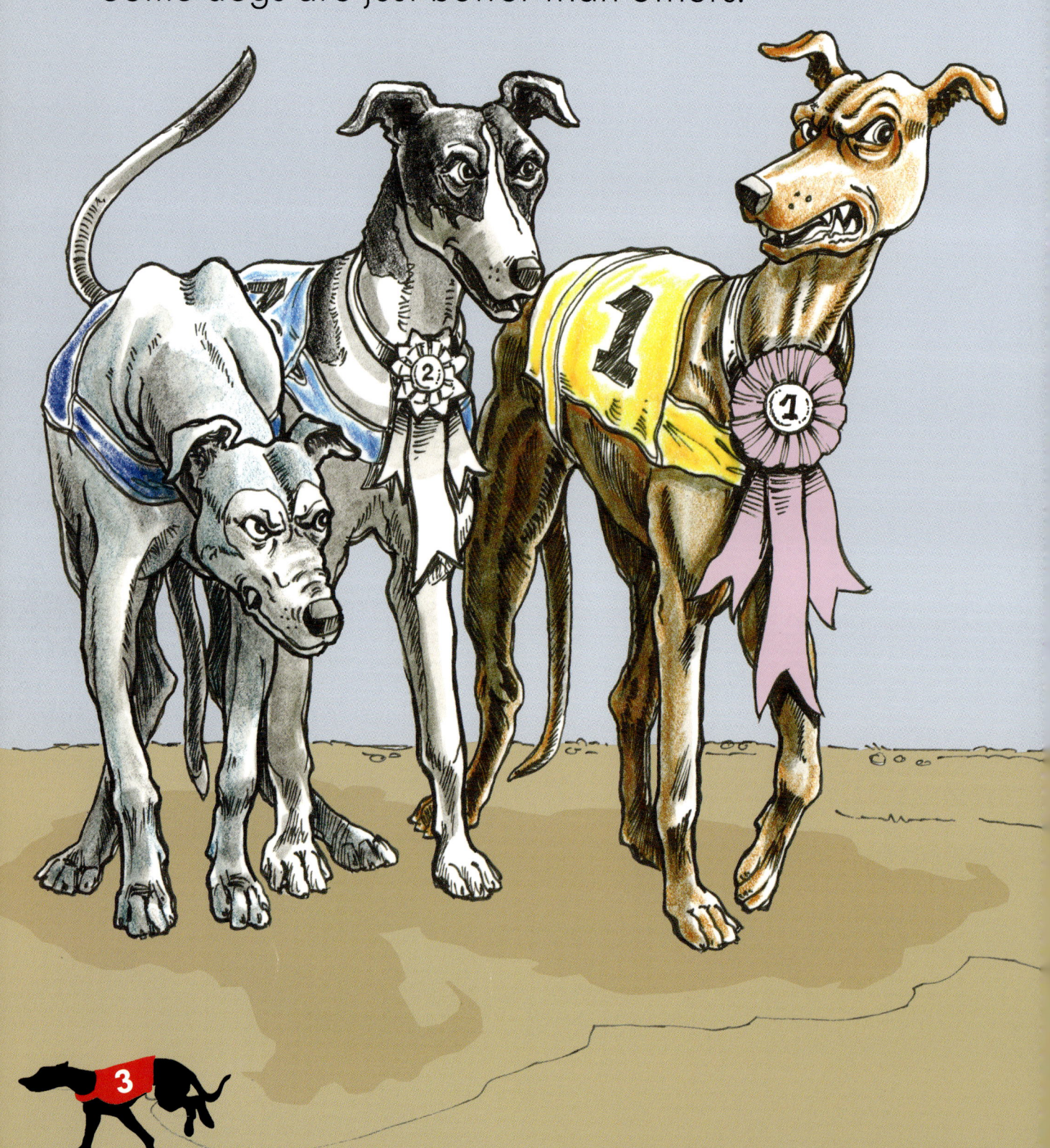

Bullet laughs and yips, "Someone has to come in last, Slowpoke. Thanks for making me look good!"

"Wimpy Legs makes all of us look good!" barks Lightning.

Streak snarls, "You just do not belong here, loser!"

I feel bad about myself when the other dogs tease me and call me names, but I do not want them to see how much their words hurt my feelings.

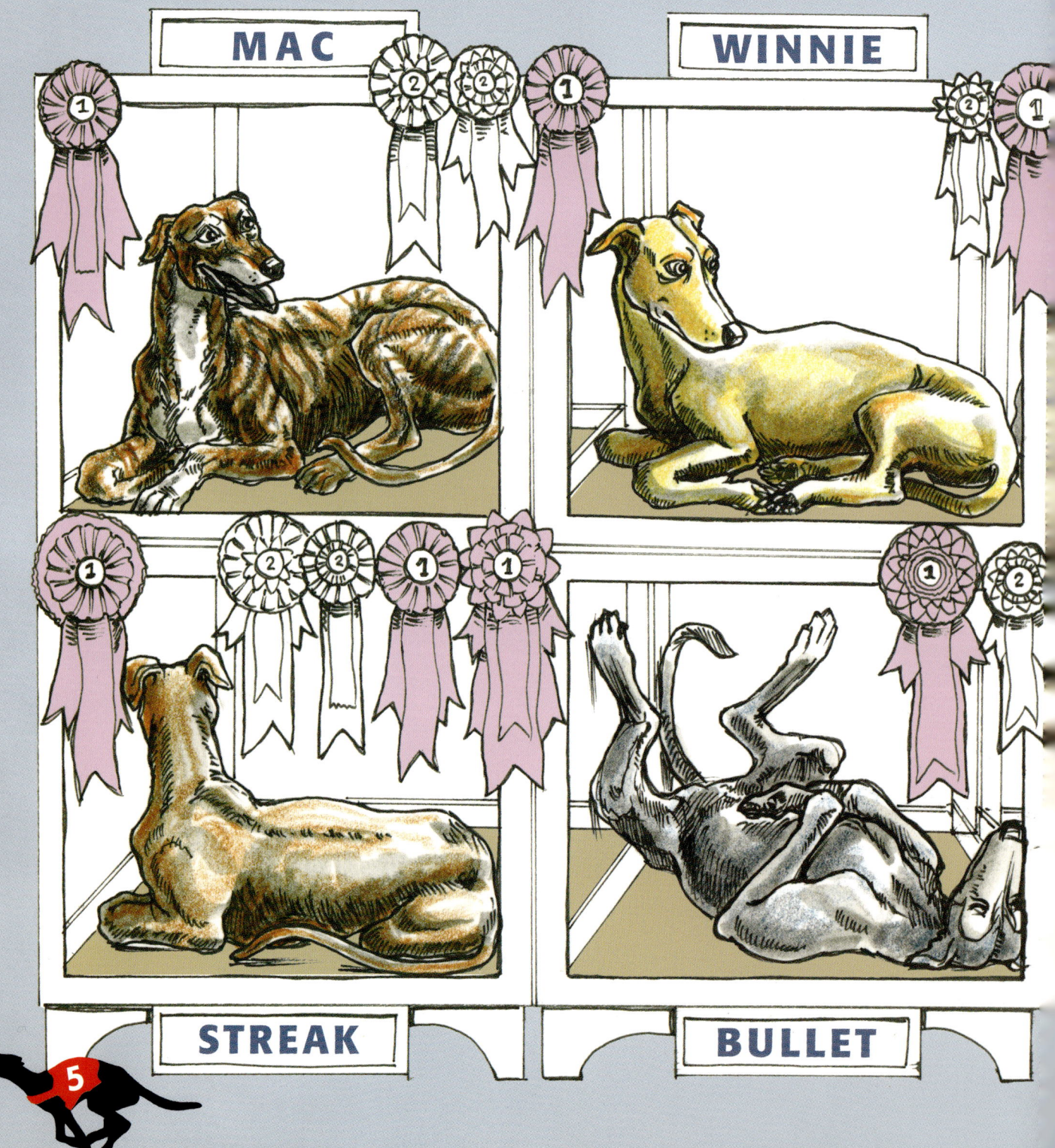

I just hide my head and cry.
Sometimes I get a tummyache.

I try to remember the times when I won a few races.

I tell Mac and Winnie how I feel.

"I feel sad and I do not
want to race and lose anymore."
Mac says, "Someday you will find a job
you can do — a place where you belong!"

Winnie whispers,

"Do not feel sad, YolandaBaby.
You always do your best.
Good dogs keep trying hard.
You just ignore the rest."

Winnie and Mac
are my good friends.
They make me feel better.

I wonder what job I am good at?
I'm thinking what it might be;
I want to feel good about myself —
I want to be a winner at being me!

One day my trainer, Timothy Tyler, says, "YolandaBaby, you are not going to race anymore. You try so hard, but you are not fast enough."

"Look at Suzette," says Timothy. "She is going to a farm to learn to be a pet. That will be her new job.

She will be adopted and live in a new home. That will be your new job, too!"

When it is time for me to leave the track,

Timothy's words make me feel better:

"YolandaBaby, you are going to be a real winner at your new job!"

I just need to think positively about being a good pet! So I repeat to myself:

"I will think positively every day, and I will be a winning pet; no racing anymore for me— this is the best job I could get!"

"YolandaBaby, this is your new trainer, Rosetta," Timothy tells me.

"Hello there, Yolanda. I brought your friend Suzette to greet you," says Rosetta.

I am glad to see Suzette, and I ask her, "Will my new trainer take care of me? Will she feed me and teach me to be a pet?"

"Yes!" yips Suzette.

Suzette yelps happily, "I cannot wait. I have been chosen to live in the city with Mrs. Crinkle. She told me about all the shops and restaurants!

I am going to be a good pet for her. I am so excited about my new job!"

"I am a good dog, Suzette," I answer. "I will be chosen, too!"

On a bright, sunny afternoon — visitors' day — Mr. and Mrs. Bippers come to the farm looking for a special pet. As Rosetta shows them all of the dogs, Murphy and Spider start showing off and barking wildly, while Poochie and Samuel hide shyly behind Rosetta.

I am on my best behavior. I walk tall and proud. I stand still and nuzzle Mr. Bippers' hand.

Mr. Bippers says, "This is a fine-looking dog. She looks like a winner to me." Mrs. Bippers exclaims, "Let's take her home!"

Rosetta says, "YolandaBaby, you are being adopted by Mr. and Mrs. Bippers. You will be their pet and live in their home."

Being their dog *is* my new job, they say.
I am excited, and life is good;
I want to please them, so I will try hard
to do all the *things* I should.

Mr. and Mrs. Bippers talk to me during the long car ride home.

I am proud of what I did today.
I have a new family and I belong.
Now all my tomorrows will be bright—
I'm feeling so happy and strong!

When we arrive home, there are lots of people and pets to welcome me.

Alex, the poodle, gives me a yellow leash and two collars — a green one for everyday and a red one for special occasions.

McCall, the big Siamese cat, brings me a soft green mouse.

Tommy, the terrier, offers a yellow duck that squeaks.

Topsy, the Sheltie, presents me with a bright green bowl for food. Dresden, the white German shepherd, gives me a bright blue bowl for water.

Friends are better than racing ribbons!

This has been such a wonderful day —
I made some new and special friends.
Perhaps they can come and play again
and the fun will never end!

Winnie and Mac were right.
I did find the job that was right for me.
I am a winner.

I am a dog who is a special pet and gives love.
This is what I was always meant to be.

About the Author

Jo Ann Bennett-Boltinghouse adopted YolandaBaby through Greyhound Pets of America. Jo Ann's learning adventure with her new family pet gave rise to combining her self-esteem background into this children's book. A self-esteem educator, Jo Ann's mission in life is "to help people be better at what they do, no matter what that may be." She is an educator, trainer, speaker, and grandmother. She resides in Iowa with her husband, Earl, and YolandaBaby. When Jo Ann isn't teaching or writing, she can be found curled up with a great book and a bowl of popcorn, enjoying world-wide travel with family and friends, or creating new ideas for interacting with her grandchildren.

About The Ginger Press

This is the first in a series of children's books about YolandaBaby's adventures in self-esteem. Due to overwhelming enthusiasm for the first book, the story was revised and newly illustrated into a second printing. Future books in this series will deal with the feelings children have as they identify with YolandaBaby's experiences. These books will address going to school, the death of a friend, a new baby in the family, and other emotionally charged situations. "I am special. You are special. We can be special together" is the resounding objective of the book series to teach children and encourage parents.

About the Illustrator

Bringing YolandaBaby from a sketch through to the final image was a labor of love. Owning two large dogs of her own, Jenniffer Julich is perfectly matched with the author as illustrator for this book. When Jenniffer isn't drawing in her studio, she too can be found educating the public, either reenacting 1750's battles at historic forts in the northeastern states or in the maple sugar bush in southern Ontario. Jnnffr (her pen name) is married with two children and lives beside historic second Welland Canal in St. Catharines, Ontario.

About YolandaBaby

YolandaBaby was born on May 17, 1998, and trained to race at the track. Although she won a few races, she was not fated to be a champion. When you are built for speed but cannot win, what else do you do?

The interactive website **www.yolandababy.com** allows you to take YolandaBaby for a walk on the path to self-esteem.

What Professionals Are Saying...

"*YolandaBaby* is the fun, whimsical tale of a greyhound (dog) whose experiences, feelings, and adventures are those any child can identify with.

This book is a wonderful asset to my therapy practice, as it identifies feelings of low self-esteem, the experience of bullying, and identity confusion. God has created us all differently, with different gifts and abilities, and when we finally fulfill the role we were created for, we experience joy, peace, and happiness.

This book can poignantly demonstrate how our self-esteem and self-confidence grows when we are met with unconditional love and acceptance from those who care for us."

Lisa A. Pattison, Ph.D.
Licensed Clinical Psychologist
Grand Island, NE

"In this story Jo Ann shares with her readers the lesson that in the race for success, only our own negative self-image can defeat us.

The most important thing you can do for your children or grandchildren is to offer them stability, guidance, and support while they explore and learn to realize the unique potential self which is unfolding within them.

If you consistently and lovingly give them positive reinforcement, they are far more likely to achieve the expectations you set for them."

Lou & Diane Tice,
authors and
business coaches
The Pacific Institute
Seattle, WA

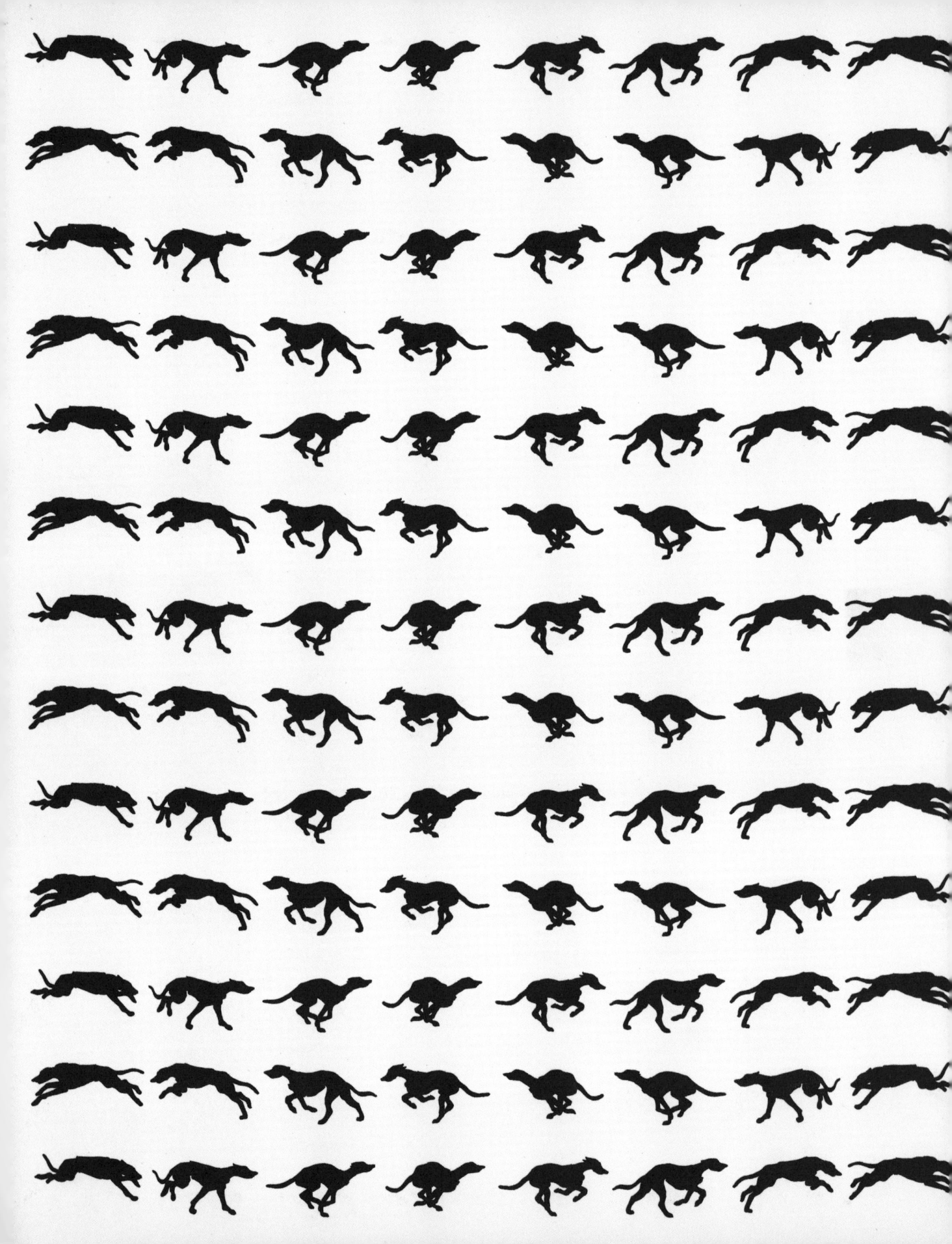